ReVamping the Librarian

Mia Harlan and Cali Mann

Contents

Chapter   1

1. Janet   3

2. Archie   10

3. Janet   16

4. Janet   21

5. Archie   27

6. Janet   36

7. Janet   42

8. Archie   47

9. Epilogue: Janet   52

About the Authors   57

Also By Cali Mann   58

Also By Mia Harlan   60

This librarian is about to get . . . revamped!

She's a lonely librarian in a small town library.
He's a vampire, who abdicated his kingdom, and is ready to walk into
the sun
But when a magic book throws her into his path,
both their lives change forever.

ReVamping the Librarian is a paranormal romantic comedy that contains certain topics that may be difficult for some readers:
Suicidal ideation, including characters contemplating whether to let
harm come to them.

Janet

♥

With a sigh, I cross my quiet little library and stop in the romance section. Who would have thought that being a librarian would be so lonely? When I took this job, I had visions of children's story hours and senior book clubs like in the library where I grew up. But not in this tiny town. It's just me and Page, the scruffy cat I found under the front porch last week. And since they gave me a basement apartment under the renovated library, I hardly ever have to leave work.

"I like to think of it as getting paid to exercise," I tell the black ball of fur. I do a few lunges to prove my point, and Page attacks my shoelaces, getting a workout of his own.

"I know what you're going to say, Page. One..." I count as I switch to squats and pitch my voice low, like what I imagine Page's would be if he could talk. "You should be recommending books to patrons and reading to little kids, Janet."

Dropping into another squat, I raise my voice an octave. "Two. And you'd be right. This is definitely not how I envisioned my librarian career would go. But at least I have plenty of free time... Three! And I get paid to read and work out."

I switch to pushups.

"Not that I get paid that much—*one*." I grunt. "But I get to live here rent-free—*two*—and in a year, I'll have saved up enough to go to Paris. *Three*. It's been my dream since I was little. *Four*. And I have you, Page. *Five*." Though I can't help silently wishing for someone human to share my life with.

I get to my feet, workout complete. What? I may not be athletic, but I make up for it with my knowledge of literature. Not that I get to use it all that often.

"I wonder if anyone will come in today." I scoop up the cat and head towards the large front window. It overlooks the wide fields that spread around the library. Sometimes, it feels like I'm the only person out here in the middle of nowhere. It's no wonder the library rarely gets any patrons.

"Between you and me, I think my trial of opening the library at 5 a.m. isn't going to work out," I tell Page. "I've been doing it for a month now, and so far, no one has taken advantage of the early hours. Maybe I should start a book club again. I know it was just me, but it's been a few months, and things change." Except maybe not out here...

For a split second, I see myself with my back stooped, and my hair gray, still stuck in this little library, living this half-life and reminding myself I should be grateful that I have a steady income and a roof over my head.

I stare out into the night. The full moon illuminates the empty roads, and I can just make out the abandoned old mansion at the edge of town. It's rumored to be haunted, but I've never believed such tales. Supernatural things only exist in books.

I scratch Page behind the ear and head back to the romance section. "Other people may not read library books anymore, but I do. What do you think? Paranormal or classic?"

Page lets out an adorable little meow.

"Classic it is. I'll just be a minute and then I'll get you some cat food. You're all skin and bones, my friend, but we're going to fix that. I've got a yummy can of tuna-flavored—"

Page yowls and jumps out of my arms, then races toward the stairs that lead to our basement apartment. His little claws click on the hardwood, a reminder that he's owed a post-breakfast claw trimming. I'm not sure if we've reached the kitty manicure stage in our seven-day relationship, but I might as well find out. It's not like I've got anything better to do, or anyone better to do it with.

I peruse the shelf of classics. It's filled with paperbacks, interspersed with donated, hand-bound, brown leather tomes that have gorgeous, gold-embossed writing on their spines. I have no idea where those donations come from, but each month, someone leaves a book or two on the library's front steps. We just got *Pride and Prejudice* this week, and I decide to re-read the old favorite.

Reaching out, I touch the spine, but before I can pull the book off the shelf, it glows with a strange purple light.

"I'm hallucinating," I mutter, knowing full well that Page is out of earshot, and I'm basically talking to myself at this point. "This is not happening. Books don't glow. Maybe I fell asleep reading, and this is all just a weird dream."

I blink and get sucked into a whirlpool of light. It yanks me straight into the bookshelf and spits me out in front of the so-called haunted mansion at the edge of town, the closest building to my little library. The dark building looms over me with its Victorian architecture and empty windows. Around me, there are surprisingly well-groomed rose bushes, and they smell wonderful—their floral fragrance is strong and robust in the night air. I guess I always thought this place was abandoned, but clearly someone tends to it.

"I'm definitely dreaming," I mutter under my breath. But if this is a dream, then why do I feel the cold wind on my bare arms? And why is my stomach roiling like I'm about to throw up?

"Everything's going to be fine. I'm okay," I mutter, turning away from the not-so-creepy mansion. "I'll just walk back to the library. Yup, that's exactly what I'll do. And then I'll pretend none of this ever happened."

"None of what ever happened?" a deep voice says from behind me.

I startle and spin around to face the man who somehow materialized on the mansion's front porch. A porch that looks like it was recently renovated, I might add.

"Did you touch a glowing book, too?" I ask, because he definitely wasn't there a few seconds ago.

"No?" It sounds like more of a question, and his eyebrows knit in adorable confusion.

Tall, dark, and handsome... and in a tailored black suit, he looks like he could have stepped out of one of my favorite classic reads. His piercing gaze and angular jaw do something funny to my insides, and I let my eyes fall, taking in the muscular frame evident even beneath his clothes. I have a sudden urge to fan myself. Is he a Heathcliff or a Mr. Darcy, though?

I shake myself. He completely contrasts with my own outfit—sweatpants and a t-shirt that says 'I like big books and I cannot lie.'

He looks me over, his eyes glinting with amusement. His lips curve up slightly in a small smile, as if he's laughing at me.

"What? I was exercising at the library," I tell him, pointing at my shirt. "It's my favorite workout shirt. And it is a whole lot less weird than walking around in a suit at this time of the morning."

"Fair enough." His deep voice sends shivers down my spine. His dark brown eyes hold mine.

My gaze shifts briefly to his lips before snapping back up. My heart is racing. "You're too attractive to be real," I tell him, then pinch my arm. "Ouch!"

"Did you just pinch yourself?"

"Maybe." I look him up and down. His chest looks solid, and I bet he's got huge pecs and rock-hard arms. I long to reach out and find out for myself. I lick my lips. "Are you sure you're real?"

"Pretty sure." He chuckles. "Unless I imagined the last 400 years of my life."

I roll my eyes at his joke. "You're not helping. I think I'm losing my mind. I'm not supposed to be here."

"Or maybe," he drawls, "you're exactly where you should be."

His voice pulls me in, his words enveloping me in a cozy cocoon. Which lasts for a solid two seconds until I remember where I am, and how I got here.

"This isn't what I meant when I said I wanted a little bit more excitement in my life," I mutter. "I was hoping for a few patrons, a good book to read, or a trip to Paris. I did not mean that I wanted to end up in a straitjacket." I shake my head. "I am definitely going crazy."

"You're not crazy," he says softly.

"But I am. Five minutes ago, I was at the library, about to feed my cat." My heart squeezes at the thought of poor, hungry Page pacing in front of his bowl, waiting for me to come downstairs.

"Why would you be feeding your cat at the library? It's not even open."

"You haven't heard about the new hours?"

The confusion on his face is answer enough.

"I put flyers in the general store, hardware store, and the post office!"

He shrugs.

"The library is open at 5 a.m. now, bright and early. Though no one's been showing up." I cross my arms in front of my chest. "Come to think of it, I've never seen you at the library. Why's that?"

"The hours don't work for me. Though now that I know you're open before sunrise, I think I'll start dropping by."

"Really?"

He nods.

I perk up. Eye candy like this guy would certainly make my mornings more exciting, and I can't help wanting to get to know him a little better. What is he doing at the mansion in a suit at this time of day?

"I take it you're the librarian?" he asks.

"I am. And that's how I ended up out here. I touched a library book, it started to glow, and then..." I grimace. "I know how crazy I sound. Obviously, you don't believe me."

"Why wouldn't I believe you?" he asks, like he frequently sees people teleporting after touching books. That cinches it: I'm losing my mind.

"I should be getting back," I say. "Not that I'm missing much. We never get any patrons." I roll my eyes. "I bet I could be gone a week and literally no one would notice."

"You know, you really shouldn't be saying things like that to a vampire you just met."

"Vampire." I snort. "Good one."

"It's not a joke." He opens his mouth, and sharp fangs pop out.

I gasp and take a step back.

He pops his fangs back in.

"I'm definitely going insane," I say, then pinch myself ten times, hoping one of them will take, and I'll finally wake up. But despite my best efforts, I can't convince myself it's all a dream. My arm stings, I'm outside the haunted mansion, and the hot man in front of me just showed me his fangs.

Archie

♥

"I did not just see fangs," the gorgeous librarian complains as she paces back and forth in front of me.

Since she did just see fangs—mine, to be exact—I choose to stay silent and let her process. Especially since it gives me the perfect opportunity to devour her with my eyes, wishing I had my lips on her, tasting her.

She looks adorable in her bookish t-shirt. It hides her curves, leaving everything to the imagination, and the words on the front make me smile... and wonder just how big she likes her books, and her men. Though now is probably not the time to find out. Not when she looks like she's about to jump out of her skin.

"How could I have been there?" She groans. "Then here?"

"It's going to be okay," I say. "You're not hurt. You're safe."

"But—" She looks back toward the library all the way on the other side of the fields. Her heartbeat picks up its pace, and I place a soothing hand on her arm.

"You know where you are," I say. "And your little library is right there. It'll barely take any time to get back."

Even less time at vampire speed, but I refrain from telling her that.

"But magic? I mean, what the hell?" There are tears glimmering at the edge of her eyes. "I've never experienced anything like this before." She looks up at me, eyes wide. "This shouldn't be happening."

She's confused and starting to fly off the handle, and I'm not sure what to do. Good thing my knight, Freddie, isn't here, or he'd be laughing his ass off. Four hundred years, give or take, and a crying woman can still make me lose my cool.

"It's okay," I say, reaching for her arms and rubbing them up and down. I certainly can't leave her, not that I would want to. There's something about her that draws me in. Something I'm not sure I'm ready to examine. She's pretty, with warm brown hair and gorgeous blue eyes that I could get lost in, but it's more than that. Though I can definitely appreciate that her body is soft in the way modern women don't like. She's got curves that a man can take hold of when he—Where is my brain going? She's crying and I'm thinking about taking her?

"What's your name?" I ask, moving closer. She's trembling, and I can hear her heart racing even faster.

"Janet," she chokes out.

I lift her chin, trying to get her to meet my eyes. Maybe I can compel her to calm down.

Her sky-blue eyes meet mine, and I am lost. I haven't seen that shade in forever. Not since before I was turned, and it's so beautiful. Vague memories of frolicking in green fields and chasing butterflies run through my mind, and I shake myself.

"Well, Janet, you're safe here," I say, forgetting all about compelling her. "I may be a vampire, but I would never harm you." Or anyone else. I did terrible things in my past, but I set aside the monarchy, and I'm living my last years as I choose. Though the thought of stepping into the sunlight and putting a stop to my endless existence is suddenly a little less appealing.

"I'm going nuts," she says, her eyes darting around the garden. "Glowing books, vampires—How did I get here?"

She's repeating herself, and her shaking worsens. I have to do something to interrupt her spiral. There's only one thing I can do.

I lean down and press my lips to hers. She's so soft and full of life. My body reacts in ways it hasn't in a long time. Her arms come around me, warm against my cold skin. I deepen the kiss. She tastes of mint and coffee, a heady combination. And when I finally feel her body relax against mine, I'm gone.

Grabbing her waist, I tug her closer. Grinding my hips against her, I groan and cup the back of her head. My fangs descend, and I instantly pull back. She sways into me, completely unaware. I don't want the kiss to end—I want more—but even I recognize we're moving too fast.

I take a step back and wait for my fangs to retract while I look her over. She seems better, but I keep my mouth closed over my fangs, just in case.

It floors me, the effect this one kiss has had on me. I hadn't believed there was anything left for me among the living. I'd been searching for a new reason to live every day and coming up short. I'd been prepared to walk into the sun any day now, but all I want to do is pull her into my arms and kiss her again.

Instead, I ask, "Are you okay?"

She takes a few deep breaths. "I'm better now, but I still don't understand."

"Not everything is meant to be understood," I say, then quote, "There are more things in heaven and earth, Horatio, than are dreamt of in your philosophy."

"Shakespeare? Really?" she asks, and a smile curves her lips.

I raise my hands. "I enjoyed that play when it was performed."

"At the festival?" she says. "I saw Hamlet there a few years ago."

I chuckle. "I preferred Hamlet at Drury Lane in the 1700s." Hopefully, now that she's more calm, I won't upset her more, though I really don't know why I'm telling her all this.

She looks amused. "There's no way you saw it then."

"Vampire," I say, gesturing toward myself. "Four hundred years or so."

She gives me a side eye that is more cute than threatening. "Even if I experienced some weird episode—maybe I sleepwalked or whatever—there's no way vampires are real. The fangs must have been a trick or something."

I grin and can't seem to resist showing her my fangs again. "You don't believe I'm a vampire?"

Janet straightens her back and glares at me like an irritated schoolmarm. "Nope."

I let my hunger show in my eyes, knowing they are turning red. "How about now?"

She frowns. "How did you do that?"

I turn and sprint up and down the garden with vampiric speed. With my enhanced hearing, I catch her soft gasp and sharp inhale.

I race to her and pull her into my arms again. She stares up at me, eyes wide, but she feels like she belongs here. I breathe her in. She smells like apple blossoms.

"That seems like normal human speed to you?"

She swallows. "You really are a vampire?"

I grin, leaving my fangs out. Her nearness is doing something to me, something that I haven't felt in a long time. I'm barely distracted by the pump of blood through her arteries, and instead focus on the soft plumpness of her lips.

She licks them and tries to step away. I tighten my hold. "I won't hurt you," I insist. "I'll never hurt you."

"Then let me go," she murmurs.

I do, and she backs toward the garden gate, as far away from me as she can get. That hurts a little, but I have to remember that she's human. There was a day I've almost forgotten—a day four centuries ago—when I discovered a world I wasn't ready for. I have to remember that.

Janet takes a few unsteady breaths. "Okay, vampires are real."

I try not to look too menacing. "I'm Archibald LaVere," I say, offering my hand. "Archie to my friends."

She looks at my hand dubiously. "Janet Collins."

"Pleased to meet you."

She shifts from side to side, looking down at the stone path. "A real vampire."

"Yes," I repeat. "I know it's hard for humans to understand."

Her sky-blue eyes meet mine again. "Have you been to Paris?"

I smile, keeping my fangs inside. "The City of Love is beautiful. I love the Eiffel Tower. The view is tremendous, especially at night with all of Paris sparkling."

She looks wistful. "I've never been. And I've always wanted to."

"Maybe I can take you sometime," I say, and immediately regret it.

I may be drawn to Janet in a way I haven't felt before, but I shouldn't be making promises. Not when I've been planning my death for over a year now. If she hadn't popped up in front of my home today, I may have gone through with it. I'd been seriously considering it. How can I promise this vivacious woman something like that if I don't know if I will be around to do with her? What if the novelty wears off and I step into the sun?

"To Paris?" she asks, her eyes shining.

"And who knows where your magic book will take you," I mention, sidestepping the question.

"Oh," she says. "I hadn't thought of that. I mean, if it really is magic, it might take me anywhere!"

She's so enthusiastic that I wonder, would seeing the world through her eyes give me new life? I've been so set on my fate, but I am beginning to glimpse another possibility now.

"Would it be all right if I walked you home?"

She nods. "I really should be getting back. Page is probably starving."

I offer her my arm, and to my surprise, she takes it.

Janet

♥

I can't stop sneaking glances at Archie as we walk along the side of the road. It's sweet of him to offer to escort me home... even if he is a vampire who doesn't own a car because he never learned to drive. Apparently, he never saw the need.

"Are there other kinds of creatures?" I ask. I can't believe I've just accepted that he's a vampire, but there's no other way to explain the fangs, red eyes, and super-speed.

"Creatures?" Archie raises an eyebrow, but my gaze drops down to his lips. I've never been kissed like that—like I'm the center of a man's universe. I've never felt the magic that was kissing Archie, and I can't help craving more.

I know I should be upset that he only kissed me to shut me up, but I can't stop thinking about the feel of his lips on mine—hard, demanding, making me forget that I had somehow magically teleported from the library to his house.

"Werewolves? Mermaids? Fairies? Are they real?"

"Yes," he says simply. "Though many of them have retired from the human world. The fae, for example, haven't interacted with humans in centuries."

I blink, unsure of how to process that information. Still, the world seems a lot more exciting knowing there were so many other kinds of creatures in it. I push on to safer subjects, if there is such a thing.

"So you're about four hundred?"

He nods. He walks close to me, and our hands are nearly brushing. Despite my brain whirling at a million miles a minute, my body is definitely reacting to his. I want to reach out and take his hand, but that seems too forward. We just met, and he's a freaking vampire. I'm not even sure he's interested—or available.

"Are you married?" I ask.

"I wouldn't have kissed you if I were." Archie lifts his gaze and focuses on the horizon, where the barest slivers of the sunrise are peeking through. "But I was, a long time ago. When I was human. But I've been alone for many years now."

His voice is so sad that I find myself reaching out and taking his hand, then squeezing it in sympathy.

"I'm sorry," I say. "You don't have to talk about it."

"It's okay. I don't mind." He pauses, and for a second, I don't think he's going to say anything, but then he adds, "Those were different times. The marriage was arranged, and I hardly knew her before she fell ill. The plague," he adds. "We'd been married less than a year. If I had stayed human, I'd likely have remarried. Had children. But I was turned before any of that could happen."

"Vampires can't have children?" I ask, wondering if that bit of lore is true.

"We cannot. But I've sired many vampires. Turned them," he adds, even though I already know what he means. He looks down at our interlocked fingers, then back at the horizon. "The sun is rising."

"Oh," I say, following his gaze. "Can you be out in the sun?"

He shakes his head, then pulls me closer. "Do you trust me?"

I shouldn't. I just met him, and he's an actual vampire, but I say, "Yes."

He scoops me into his arms and runs at full speed to the library. My breath whooshes out of me, and I close my eyes at the blur of landscape. The slightest bit of smoke rises off him as he sets me on the porch. It takes me a second to get my bearings, and I lean against him unsteadily.

"Do I need to invite you in?" I ask.

"No. But I'd appreciate it if you could unlock the front door." More smoke rises from his skin.

"It's unlocked. The library opens—"

Archie pulls the door open and zooms inside.

"—at five," I mutter under my breath. "Maybe I need to get a large, neon 'open' sign."

I follow Archie inside. Tiny paws scamper up the steps, and Page appears. He races straight for our visitor, and I lurch forward to stop him. But the little ball of fur rushes right between my legs and launches himself at Archie. I expect my pet to claw the vampire, but Page settles comfortably on the man's shoulder.

"I'll take him before he ruins your suit."

"It's fine." Archie chuckles, patting Page like he's used to cats climbing him. Maybe he is.

"Are vampires some sort of cat magnets?"

"Not that I know of." He runs his fingers through Page's fur. "Who's an adorable little kitty? You are."

I can't help grinning as I introduce them. "Page, say hello to Archie." My cheeks flush as I belatedly remember Page is a cat and can't talk. "Archie, this is Page. I found him under the porch last week when I was taking out the trash."

Page meows, almost as if to say hello.

"Nice to meet you," Archie says, and I'm not sure if he talks to cats, too, or if he's just humoring me. Either way, any reservations I've had about inviting a vampire into this isolated library dissolve. Not that he actually needed to be invited in.

"Can I look around?" Archie asks. "I'd love to see the library."

I nod. "It's a *public* library. Everyone is welcome."

"Including vampires?" he teases.

I nod. "Would you like a tour?" I glance at the fiction section and quickly look away. What if we pass by *Pride and Prejudice* and it sends me to Alaska or the middle of the ocean?

"A tour would be wonderful."

"I just need to feed Page first. The little guy must be starving." I lead the way across the foyer toward the stairs. "Thank you so much for walking me home. I really appreciate it."

He smiles. "Are you okay with letting me stay for the day? The sun's up now, and I won't be able to make it back to the manor easily." He actually looks uncomfortable.

"Will the sunlight kill you?"

"Not immediately. I could get back in time, but it would hurt."

"Then, yes, you can stay." My heart pounds at the thought. I glance at Page, snuggled on his shoulder. "I don't think my cat is letting you go any time soon."

Archie chuckles and follows me downstairs. My apartment is tiny and a bit embarrassing, but it's mine.

"I'm sorry your breakfast is late, bud," I say as I open a can of food for the purring Page.

"This is where you live?" Archie asks, looking around.

"The apartment comes with the job."

Archie nods and runs his fingers along some of the handmade throw blankets I've collected over the years. "I love their bright colors."

I smile. "My mother made these. She loved crafting, but especially making throws. A color for every mood." The familiar sense of loss settles in the pit of my stomach, but it's the first time I've had the chance to talk about her since she passed, and the words flood out. "Chilly evenings were her favorite. We would each pick a throw, and I'd snuggle with a good book while she'd work on her next creation. She always said how she loved the interplay of colors and textures."

"They're beautiful," he says. "So lively."

I can't help the snort that escapes me. A vampire calling something lively. Then I shake myself.

"Cat's fed. So... Let's go upstairs," I say. "I'll give you that tour."

Janet

♥

Archie and I head back to the library, and he turns straight toward the classics. My heart leaps into my throat.

"Stop!" I shout.

Archie freezes and glances at me, eyebrows raised.

"Don't go near Pride and Prejudice. Not until we're sure it won't teleport you somewhere."

"So that's the culprit?" Archie chuckles.

"You laugh now, but what if it dumps you in the middle of the field in broad daylight?"

"Point taken." He changes direction.

I show him the non-fiction section and take him through the other fiction aisles, then end our tour at the board games.

"That's unusual," Archie says, taking them in.

"I thought it might bring in patrons." I sigh, staring at the brand new, unused boxes.

"I haven't heard of most of these," Archie says, perusing the titles and stopping in front of the chess set. "Do you play?"

I shake my head. "I've always wanted to learn."

"I play chess with Freddie once a week," he says.

"Freddie?" I can feel my eyebrows rising.

"My knight."

"Not your friend?" I ask.

"Well, I guess so," he says, shifting uncomfortably. "As king, I didn't really have any friends."

"As king?" I ask, my voice rising.

He nods but doesn't elaborate. Is he a king? Or was he a king? My thoughts whirl, but I try to push it out of my mind. He'll tell me when he's ready.

He settles on the couch, as far from the window as possible. It's meant for patrons who come to the library to read, but I'm the only one who's ever sat there in the two years since I got hired.

I thought Archie would look out of place in the library, especially in his suit, but he seems at home. He leans back, his arms resting on the back and side of the small sofa.

"Do you need to sleep the sleep of the dead?" I ask, half-joking.

"No," he says. "I'm old enough that I don't sleep much. Five, maybe six hours, but a bit of extra blood fixes that."

"Blood..." I whisper, a rock settling in the pit of my stomach. "Do you... need to feed?"

Archie chuckles. "I'm not going to bite you, Janet. Not unless you ask me to."

Something about the way he says it makes my heart race, and I suddenly can't stop picturing his lips on my neck, his fangs buried inside me.

"You're safe with me," Archie says. "I give you my word."

I nod. "You don't need to bite someone? So you don't starve?"

He shakes his head. "There are blood banks now. I have a stash back home, and I just ate. It should tide me over for a day or two."

"Okay, then." I settle next to him, my heart pounding. Now that I'm no longer thinking about being bitten, I wonder if he'll kiss me again, and my gaze drifts down to his lips.

They move. "What kind of books do you like to read, Janet?"

"Mostly romance and classics." Which is probably the only kissing I'll be seeing. I doubt he'll kiss me again. He only did it that first time because I'd been about to cry.

"Who are your favorite authors?"

I list off a few classics, and then a few romance authors, and Archie nods like he knows what I'm talking about.

"Do you read romance?" I ask skeptically.

He nods, and his cheeks take on a red tint. "Vampires have a lot of time on our hands."

I'm still not convinced. "What's your favorite romance book?"

Archie gets to his feet and heads towards the romance section. He starts to reach for a book, spots the classics farther back, and detours.

"Wait," I cry after him.

"I promise I won't touch Pride and Prejudice, or any glowing books," Archie assures me.

I swallow, nod, and follow him. There isn't much I'll be able to do if a book sends us on a trip, but I can't stomach the thought of Archie teleporting out of my life for good. Plus, there's always a chance that this time, we'll end up in Paris.

Archie almost makes it to the romance section before he changes his mind and turns to the classics. He stops and surveys the shelf. "Pride and Prejudice isn't here."

"It isn't?" I step up next to him. He's right. All the other beautifully bound editions are there, but not Pride and Prejudice. "I don't suppose someone came in while I was out?"

He shrugs. "Maybe it disappeared when you teleported? One magical use only?"

I nibble on my lip.

"I'm glad you've kept my donations," he continues.

"Your donations?" My eyes widen. "Wait, you're the one who's been buying these for the library?"

He traces his fingers along the spines. "Making them, actually."

My jaw drops. "You're making them? How?"

"I was a bookbinder before I was turned." He rubs the back of his neck. "I've missed it, so I set up my own printing press at home."

"Those take way more than a printing press. They're masterpieces."

"It's kind of you to say so."

"I'm serious. Books like that..." I wave my hand vaguely, at a loss for words.

"Thank you," he says softly. "I've really missed the craft. The hand-sewn binding, page trimming, lettering, the designs." He sighs. "Modern paperbacks just don't have the same feel."

"Is that why you've been making classics?"

He shakes his head. "I only create titles that are out of copyright. I considered getting permission from some of my favorite authors, but that would involve asking them to send me their original manuscript."

"So who are your favorite authors?" I press. I know Archie mentioned reading romance, but I still expect him to pick up mystery or horror. He grabs a paranormal romance instead. "If I could have my pick of titles, I'd hand-bind this one. Brown leather, gold leaf wolf on the cover."

"Not a vampire book?" I chuckle.

"No. Books about vampires get so many facts wrong that I can't read them," he says, leading me back to the couch.

I can't help but agree. Now that I've met an actual vampire, I'm not sure if I'll be able to read them, either. "Do authors get werewolves right?"

Archie grins. "Can't really mess up howling at the moon, can you?"

I smile back.

"But, no. They get all the werewolf stuff wrong, too. I just find it amusing. Let me show you my favorite part," he says, taking a seat and flipping through the book.

I don't know what comes over me, but as I settle next to him, I say, "Why don't you read it to me?"

The idea of the steamy romance read aloud in Archie's voice does funny things to my insides, and I want to scoot over closer to him. I'm a librarian, and no one takes on this admittedly poorly paying career if they don't love books. I love reading them, listening to them, and seeing them acted out.

As he flips through the paperback, my heart races. And as he starts to read from the beginning of chapter nine, butterflies erupt in my stomach, and I can't help scooting closer on the couch. His voice is deep and rich, and perfect for the story. He would make an amazing audiobook narrator.

Somehow, I'm even more attracted to the man than I was before. I can barely pay attention to what he is saying. My gaze keeps drifting to his lips and his hands grazing the pages.

I've already read the book, so I know exactly where the scene is going. Archie does too, and his cheeks flush. The scene doesn't even get heated before he suddenly stops, his fingers resting lightly on the page.

Our eyes meet, and it's like we can't pull away. I don't know who leans in first, but suddenly the poor library book drops to the carpeted floor and we're reaching for each other.

When Archie's lips touch mine, it's like an explosion of fireworks. The kiss is a thousand times better than our first, which shouldn't even be possible, but somehow it is. His lips are soft and gentle on mine, but I can feel his fangs, a reminder that I'm kissing a vampire. Somehow, that only turns me on more.

Archie's arms slide around me, and I moan and grab the front of his suit jacket and hold on for dear life. I want the kiss to last forever, but as suddenly as we are together, Archie is pulling back.

He slides back on the couch, putting distance between us, and I can't help but feel hurt. Am I a terrible kisser? Did I misread his signals?

Archie

♥

My hormones are raging like a teenager, and I want nothing more than to ravish Janet right here in the middle of the library. Which is why I put distance between us, even though it's the last thing I want.

I can see the hurt in Janet's eyes, but I need a minute to think. I haven't wanted a woman like this in a long time. Hell, an hour ago, I wasn't sure I even wanted to live to see another day.

I'm terrified that I'm falling for the woman in front of me when we've only just met. It shouldn't be possible. I've heard of tales of fated mates, but only among the werewolves I've read about in books. Not real vampires, such as myself.

I brush her long hair back from her face, and her stomach growls. Her cheeks heat, and I smile at how absolutely adorable this woman looks.

"Let me make you breakfast," I say, meeting her beautiful blue eyes.

"You need to eat?" she asks, a frown line forming between her eyebrows.

I want to smooth it out. "Need? No. But vampires have enhanced taste buds, and I enjoy food." I shrug. "And I love to cook."

"What are enhanced taste buds? Do you mean everything tastes too salty or—"

"No. Everything tastes... better. I think it's the only reason I still wish to eat. I've..." I trail off before I admit that I've lost interest in everything else, including living.

In all the time I've been on this earth, I've seen everything there was to see and done everything there was to do. Hell, I sired vampires, built a kingdom, and reigned as their king.

I've done everything I thought I wanted to do, and I was sure I was done with life. But Janet makes me feel alive just by sitting here, on the couch in her library. I want to experience everything with her. To see her eyes light up with joy at every new place we see, every moment we share. I can't believe I just met this woman, and I'm already thinking about such things.

"Breakfast sounds good," she says with a small smile. "The kitchen's downstairs."

"Why don't you stay up here and relax while I cook?" I ask, handing her the paperback.

"Are you sure? I could help."

I force myself to shake my head. "I'll manage."

"In that case, I do have some work to do," she says.

I look around the empty library, and she grins.

"I don't mean around here. But that's part of the problem. Which is why I signed up for a training seminar from the ALA."

I rack my brain to figure out what the acronym stands for, but she beats me to it.

"The American Library Association. I missed it live because I mixed up the time zone, but there's a recording. I'm hoping it'll give me some ideas on how to make this place more lively."

I nod and force myself to walk away. I need some time to think about what I'm getting into here. Her cat, Page, follows me down the stairs to her basement apartment, probably hoping for a second breakfast.

"It must be nice, being a cat," I tell him.

He meows in response, almost like he understands me and is in full agreement.

"Until I met your mom, I'd been planning how I would meet my true death," I tell the cat. "What if this thing I feel for her is just a phase? I can't lead her on if I'm not even sure I'll be around. I can't risk hurting her."

Page examines one of his paws—rather judgmentally, I might add.

I grudgingly refill his dry food dish and pull open the fridge. Eggs, milk, and bread... she's got a fine start for breakfast. I dig through the cupboards to find a few spices and extras.

Page ignores the food and climbs up on the back of the couch to watch me work.

"What am I going to do?" I ask the cat as I whisk the eggs and milk. "She's not just a flirtation. Janet's someone I can see myself with forever, but I can't promise her that."

He nods sagely as if understanding every word.

"And she's a human. She won't live long." I pour the mix into the pan and add some salt and pepper. "Unless I turn her..." I freeze and stare at Page. "It's been ages since I turned anyone. Do you think she'd like being a vampire?"

"Oh, who am I kidding?" I growl to myself. "I don't even like being a vampire. I'm tired and I'm old, and if I turned her and then walked into the sun to meet my true death, she'd hate me for the rest of her endless life."

As the eggs cook, I pop the bread into the toaster. "Did I see some oranges in the fridge?"

"Meow," Page says. He hops down and comes to look in the fridge with me. He nudges an open can of tuna, and I take it out for him. A little extra for his breakfast won't hurt him.

"If I'm falling for her," I say as I scoop the tuna into a clean bowl and set it on the floor. "Does that mean fated mates are real? Is that what we are?" But those only exist in books, and only shifter books at that. "Or soulmates, perhaps?" Though that sounds equally far-fetched.

Page dives into the tuna, face first. I doubt he's even listening now, if he ever was.

"I could stay with her, while she's human," I say as I pull out the oranges. "But what happens when she dies and I'm left alone... again?" I flip through the cupboards, looking for a juicer, and find it in the back above the fridge.

"One day at a time, that's what Freddie says," I mutter. Freddie likes to come play chess with me now and then, though I'm not his king anymore.

I was going to meet the true death any day now... but maybe I could put it off for a while? See what happened with Janet first? I don't have to decide right this instant.

I finish up the eggs and set out plates and glasses on a tray. Then I serve everything and turn off the stove. I lift the tray filled with food and head for the stairs. Page meows and pads after me.

"That smells amazing," Janet says from behind the reception desk. She stands as I enter the library.

"Breakfast is served," I say with a toothy grin. I love pleasing her. She lights up when she's happy, and my entire world is brighter.

Her gaze drifts down to the tray. "That looks amazing!"

"I'm glad you like it." I glance toward a table and chairs near the front windows, where the sun is streaming in. "Is there a less bright place to eat?"

"Yes," she says, and leads me back into the stacks to a small table and chairs in the children's section. They are too small for us, so we just move the chairs aside and sit on the floor. All around us are children's books and stuffed animals. In one corner, there's a model train set made of blocks. They look dusty.

"There's really no children who use the library?" I ask, setting out our plates on the tiny table.

Janet glances around sadly. "No. Or adults. No one uses the library." She bites her lip. "Well, not exactly true. There are a handful of regular patrons. Five, really."

My brow furrows. "But then, why keep the library open? No offense."

"Someone paid for the library as their legacy," she says. "Not realizing that the town would dry up when the younger generation all moved to the city." She digs into her eggs, takes a bite, and there's that brightness again.

For a split second, I picture how much joy she'd feel tasting the food as a vampire. The moment I take a bite, flavor explodes on my tongue, and I want that for her. But I can't turn her and then abandon her... and I can't promise I'll stick around. I mentally shove away that thought and focus on the conversation.

"Was the donor Mr. Peterson?" I ask.

"Yeah," she says, then looks at me. "You knew him?"

I sip the orange juice and nod. "He was a friend."

She reaches over and rests her hand on top of mine. I look at this simple gesture of kindness and smile softly at her. "Jeb Peterson's the reason I came to this town. It's actually a funny story, how we met."

Janet takes a sip of her orange juice and waits for me to elaborate.

"You know how I said being a vampire leaves a lot of time for reading?"

She nods.

"And that I was a king once?" I say. I realize I didn't really explain it, and I'm not sure now is the time to go into all the details. I'd grown tired of ruling, just like I'd grown tired of living. "Anyway, I'm not now. I passed the mantle to someone else."

I shake my head, pressing on. "When I built my kingdom. I based it directly under the Lakeview city library." Lakeview was the nearest city, but still a three-hour drive away from here. "Our home cannot be penetrated by sunlight, or found by humans, unless they know where to look. It's safe... and, as an added perk, it allows us to borrow books at night if we're looking for something to read."

"And an endless supply of books." Janet's eyes light up. Being with her is like sitting in the sun as a human. I feel warmer, kinder, and more alive. "So you met Mr. Peterson at the library?"

"Yes, and no." I chuckle at the memory. "I'd borrowed a copy of The Great Gatsby and I'd been reading it while eating dinner."

"I do that." Janet nods in understanding.

"Well, not quite. My dinner was a blood bag. But there must have been some manufacturing defect, so it exploded all over the book."

Janet gasps. "Oh no!"

I nod. "And it wasn't just a paperback. It was a beautiful, gilded copy donated by one Jebodiah Alexander Peterson."

"Mr. Peterson," Janet says softly.

I nod. "I could have just left it alone, but I felt so bad that I tried to replicate the copy, down to the binding and gold leaf lettering. I returned the book and wrote an apology letter to Jeb. He'd been so impressed with the binding, we started corresponding. We began to meet at the Lakeview library. He'd drive in all the time until..." I trail off. Until he died.

"I'm sorry for your loss," Janet says softly.

"So am I. Jeb was a great man."

"Sounds like it." Janet nods. "I see now why he donated the library to our town. He must have really loved books."

"He did." I nod.

We lapse into a comfortable silence. Janet digs into her breakfast, and when she clears her plate, she reiterates, "This food is amazing."

"I love how you glow when you're happy," I say quietly.

She meets my eyes, and I just want to take her in my arms and kiss her again. Well, more than that. I want to hear her moan in passion.

"Thank you for breakfast." She looks off toward the front of the stacks. "And for talking with me. It's been so lonely here..."

I slide around the table and take her hands in mine. "I think we've both been lonely, and I think we could help each other be less so."

Her cheeks grow pink, but she doesn't draw her hands away.

I stroke her fingers. "I'd like to kiss you again."

She nods.

I pull her into my lap, pressing my lips to hers as I stroke her shoulders and her arms. She tastes like sunshine and light. I deepen the kiss, wanting more, wanting everything. My interest rises beneath her, and she wriggles on my lap. I growl in response, and my fang accidentally pierces her lip.

Blood wells. She draws away with a gasp and wipes the blood from her lip with her index finger. I can't help it. I take that finger and suck it into my mouth, tasting her blood.

Janet inhales sharply.

A tiny cut on a human shouldn't affect me, but somehow, I want... I don't even know what I want. Except I do. I give her finger one last lick and pull back.

"I want you, Janet," I say, my gaze locked on her lip. "I want all of you."

I let my eyes trail down her body as she gets to her feet and moves away from me. I expect to see fear on her face, but desire is reflected back at me instead.

She bites her lower lip, drawing another drop of blood, and I zoom to my feet.

As I lean in to lick the blood off her lips, Janet's pulse speeds up, and I stop abruptly. What if it's fear? I need to know for sure.

"Do you want me to stop?" I ask.

I brace myself for rejection, but she shakes her head and takes my hand in hers. She leads me downstairs to her apartment and to her bedroom. We stop in front of her bed, and she looks up at me, the tempting droplet of blood no longer on her lip.

"I want you, Archie," she says, her cheeks flushed with desire.

She reaches to pull off my suit jacket, and I shrug out of it. Her fingers tremble as she reaches for the top button of my dress shirt, but I don't have the patience. I rip it wide open.

Janet's eyes widen, and she can't seem to tear them off my abs. I can't help my grin.

I want to be patient, but my dark side roars within me, and I drop my pants. My fangs ache, and I know my eyes have turned red, but I can smell Janet's desire. I won't be able to hold myself in check much longer.

I reach for the waistband of my boxers, and Janet licks her lips. That's all the encouragement I need. I shove the material down, and my cock springs free.

Janet's cheeks flood with color. "I want you, Archie."

Her words break the last of my self-control, and I rush toward her.

Janet

♥

Archie zooms towards me at vampire speed, his fangs bared, his eyes blood-red and glued to my chest.

I barely have a chance to gasp before he grabs the collar of my bookish exercise t-shirt and shreds it. The rip of fabric is loud in the silent room.

It's one of my favorite shirts, but the fact that I'll need to order another one—or possibly five, just to be safe—is the last thing on my mind. Desire and anticipation course through me, and Archie's eyes drift down... to my old beige bra.

I cringe. Why in the name of books did I wear this thing? Then again, when I dressed this morning, the chances of me getting naked with an attractive man weren't just slim... they were non-existent. But I should have worn something less plain. Should I say something? Laugh it off? Change?

Archie freezes and takes a step back. "I'm frightening you, aren't I?"

I flounder, racking my brain for an explanation that won't leave me completely embarrassed.

Archie's gaze turns repentant. He zooms across the room with vampiric speed, moving as far away from me as the small space will allow him.

"I didn't mean to scare you," he says softly. "My fangs pop out when I'm turned on. And fuck, I want you so bad. But I would never do anything to hurt you. If you want me to stop, I will."

"I know you'd never hurt me." My cheeks flush, acutely aware of the state of undress we're both in. Archie, fully naked, and me in my worn-out bra.

I grab the edges of my torn shirt and pull it closed in front of me. Archie feels no such modesty. How is he oblivious to the fact that he's as nude as the day he was born... well, human-born? I'm not sure what he was wearing during his vampire birth, though I make a mental note to ask him. Right now, I can barely focus on anything but him.

My eyes trace down his toned chest, taking in every inch of him. His abs are perfectly defined, and a thin trail of hair runs down from his navel downward, like an arrow pointing to his huge cock, which is standing at attention... and pointing directly at me. I look away briefly, my gaze jumping to his muscular thighs. They're as huge as the rest of him. The sight makes me even wetter.

I lick my lips, my mouth watering in anticipation. I want him inside me, possessing me. I want to know what it feels like, being with a man. No, not a man. A vampire.

"You like what you see?" Archie purrs, his voice low and seductive. A smug grin spreads across his face, sending my heart racing.

I swallow and tighten the grip on my torn shirt. "I do like it," I admit. "But, Archie, you should know... I've never done this before. I want to, but..." I trail off, too embarrassed to admit that I have no clue what I'm doing.

Archie nods. "I know being with a vampire is different," he says, misunderstanding me. And why not? Who's ever heard of a virgin my age? Not in this century, anyway.

Though, considering how long the guy's lived, shouldn't he be used to virgins?

"We can take it slow. There's no rush. And I'm sorry I tore your shirt," he says.

"The reason I reacted the way I did," I press on, "isn't because it's my first time with a vampire. It's because it's my first time with anyone."

His eyes widen. "First time? Janet, are you saying that you're a virgin?"

I nod.

"Fuck."

His reply sends a flood of heat traveling up my cheeks, and I feel a sudden need to defend myself... especially since Archie's reaction makes it clear he doesn't want to do this anymore. Which isn't my fault. It's not like there have been that many opportunities to lose my virginity, especially these last few years. I haven't met a single eligible man... well, except Archie. Who, as he reminded me, isn't a man, but a vampire.

I place my hands on my hips and glare at him. "Don't blame me. I work in a library in the middle of nowhere. Before today, the youngest man I've seen in over a year was sixty-five. And library school was practically all women."

At Archie's incredulous look, I turn away from him.

"Never mind, Archie. It's fine. Let's get dressed. Clearly you were just after a random fling, and you don't want an inexperienced virgin who has no clue what she's doing. Though technically, I've read so much romance, I'd probably be a natural," I murmur.

I try to ignore the lump in my throat. Even though I've only known Archie for a short time, I feel drawn to him in a way that I've never felt with anyone before. And getting to know him, talking about our favorite books and our lives, has made me feel close to him. Like we could be friends, and maybe more. But it's more than that. It's like something primal, deep down, is telling me he's the one... Only now I know it's all in my head. I probably won't see Archie after this, and it hurts more than I'd like to admit.

"Janet, I didn't stop because I only want a fling. I stopped because I care."

I turn around to face him. His words send a surge of hope coursing through me, but I hold my breath and wait for him to say more.

"I like you, a lot, and I don't want to take your innocence. Not when you're obviously not ready."

"Of course I'm ready," I scowl at him. "I'm twenty-freaking-five, and I still haven't had sex with anyone." I realize how that makes me sound and quickly add. "And I don't want to have sex with anyone."

Archie's face falls.

"I mean with *just* anyone," I clarify. "I want to have sex with you, Archie."

His eyes instantly blaze bright red, and his fangs pop out. I love that he has such an obvious tell, and it sets my heart racing.

Archie instantly freezes. "You're scared."

"I'm not."

"Your heart's racing."

I gasp. "You can tell?"

"I can hear it."

"All the time?"

He nods.

"Great." I cross my arms over my chest. "So I can't hide how attracted I am to you?"

He grins. "You're attracted to me?"

I roll my eyes. "Like you didn't know. But at least you can't hide it either, Mr. Red Eyes and Fangs."

He chuckles. "I don't want to hide it. But I also don't want to scare you or rush you. If I'm going too fast, just say the word. We can sit, talk. We don't have to do anything you're not ready for."

"I don't want to sit or talk," I say, taking a step forward to close the distance between us. "I want you, Archie."

I place my hands on his shoulders and rise to my tiptoes to kiss him. Archie is stiff beneath my touch. He doesn't move a muscle, and when our lips touch, he doesn't kiss me back.

It's like he doesn't believe my words, and I know I need to convince him somehow. So I do the only thing I can think of. I reach behind me and unclasp my bra, letting it fall to the floor.

Archie's gaze drops to my exposed breasts, and he squeezes his hands into fists, like he's holding himself back from touching me.

I want to feel his hands on me. I crave his touch more than I've ever craved anything in my life. I *need* him.

I reach down, my palms sweating as I pull down my sweatpants and shimmy out of them and my panties, letting both fall to the floor. I'm left standing fully nude, and his gaze roves over me.

I wait for him to take the lead. To do something. Anything...

He stays perfectly still.

Okay, Janet. You've got this. You read smutty novels. You know what you're doing better than anyone!

Except my mind goes completely blank, and, like the virgin that I am, I have zero clue what to do.

Do I just reach out and grab his cock? Or is that moving too fast? It's basically the equivalent of him stepping forward and shoving a finger inside me, and no matter how much I want him, I'd like some foreplay, thank you very much.

Should I touch myself instead? I'd love to watch Archie stroke his cock, but would he enjoy watching me rub one out? Or will he think I'm some weirdo who masturbates in public?

Janet

♥

I realize I'm hyperventilating like a crazy person.

Get it together, Janet!

Not that I can blame myself for panicking.

How in all that is bookish do I get a hot-as-hell vampire to fuck the living daylights out of me when he knows I'm a virgin?

Archie's eyes widen, and my hand snaps up to my mouth. "Did I say that aloud?"

"You want me to fuck you?" Archie asks.

I nod, suddenly feeling shy. My blush reaches a brand-new level of burning inferno. "I do. I just don't know what I'm doing. This is all new to me. Can you show me what to do? Please?"

That's all the encouragement Archie needs. He scoops me up with vampiric speed and zooms across the room. Everything blurs around us, and I feel the air against my face for a split second before he deposits me in the middle of my bed.

Then he's on top of me, covering my naked body with his, and I can't help it. My whole body tenses.

There's such a thing as moving too fast, but Archie's vampirism takes it to a whole other level. What have I gotten myself into?

"Relax. I've got you," Archie whispers against my ear.

Just like that, the tension seeps out of me.

"Good girl." He plants a soft kiss on my lips. "Now, let me make you feel good."

His words make me shiver in anticipation and spread my thighs. I'm still nervous, but I want this. I want him.

Archie chuckles. "Not yet. We need to take our time. Make sure you're ready."

"I am ready."

Archie shakes his head. "Not yet."

He covers my lips with his. The kiss is slow. Luxurious. Archie takes his time exploring my mouth, and when I cup the back of his head and try to deepen the kiss, he nips at my lower lip.

I moan. Even though it doesn't sting, I'm acutely aware that he's a vampire and has fangs.

He pulls away. I grab the back of his head to pull him back, but he resists. "I've got you," he whispers, his breath warm against my lips.

He peppers soft kisses along my cheeks, then moves down to my neck. His fangs graze my sensitive skin, and I tense. "Um, Archie..."

"Yes, Janet?" he asks, running his fangs along my neck.

I shiver, partly in fear, partly in anticipation. "Are you going to bite me?"

"Not yet."

I'm only slightly disappointed. Mostly, I'm relieved. I'm nervous enough already. I'm about to have sex with a man who I'm more attracted to than anyone in the world, and I have no idea what I'm doing. I don't think I want to add biting into the equation.

Archie runs his fangs along my right breast and slides one across my nipple. I gasp, and he runs his tongue along the tip, soothing it.

I grab his muscular shoulders, then run my hands down his muscular arms. His skin is cold beneath my touch, and I can't seem to get enough.

Archie shifts his attention to my other nipple. The tip of his fang teases it, only to be replaced by his tongue. The sensations he sends coursing through me are unlike anything I've ever experienced, and I need... I need...

"More. Please, Archie, more!"

He sucks my nipple into his mouth, his fangs grazing my breast, but not piercing skin. Pleasure unlike anything I've ever known envelops me.

"Please, Archie," I beg again, arching my hips up off the bed, needing to ease the ache between my thighs.

"We've only just begun, Janet."

I whimper. "I don't know how much more I can take."

Archie pulls back. "Do you want me to stop?"

"The opposite. I want you to speed up. Use some of that vampire speed."

"Next time." He pinches my nipple, but he's gentle. Too gentle. "This time, we take it slow. Make sure you're ready."

"I am ready, and I don't want slow, Archie." I reach between us and grab his cock.

Archie lets out a hiss, which surprises me for a split second, but doesn't scare me. I stroke my hand up and down his length, reveling in the feel of him.

His red eyes bore into mine. "Are you sure you're ready for vampire speed?"

Before I can talk myself out of it, I nod. "Yes."

Suddenly, Archie's cock is no longer in my hand, and he's spreading my thighs wide, his face right at my core. I don't have time for shyness, or even time to think. His breath heats my sensitive flesh, then his tongue is on my clit.

I moan as pleasure radiates through me. I've never felt anything like this before. I don't want him to stop. Ever.

Then his finger is inside me, filling me while he licks me. His tongue is gentle but everywhere all at once, thanks to vampire tongue speed. Every nerve ending I have is on fire. Delicious pressure builds inside me. I rock my hips, chasing that feeling, and he slides another finger inside me, stretching me just a bit more.

I groan. My fingers curl in the sheets, and I cry out.

"I'm going to make you come, Janet," Archie whispers against my core and licks me again.

I squeeze around his fingers.

"All I want is to make you feel good." He groans approvingly before his vampire tongue is back.

Then he has me screaming while I shatter around his finger. I can't stop shaking and a tiny whimper escapes when Archie's hot breath grazes my oh-too-sensitive clit.

"You're so beautiful when you come," he murmurs against my clit.

He starts to slide his fingers out, then seems to change his mind and slides them in again. He flicks them up, grazing the sensitive spot inside me, and I arch my hips in surprise.

He repeats the action, again and again, until I'm clenching around his fingers and pumping my hips, whimpering with need. Then he puts his vampire speed to work again, his tongue gently grazing my folds, letting the pleasure build.

"Come for me again, Janet." His words echo through the room, along with my whimpers, as I chase my release. "Yes, just like that."

I cry out as I come, spasming around his fingers. Then they're suddenly no longer there. Archie's lips land on mine, and he kisses me.

His hard cock presses against my entrance. There's that vampire speed again.

"Last chance to change your mind," Archie whispers softly.

"I want you. Only you." I grab his hips and arch up, forcing his cock into me.

I yelp at the slight sting, and Archie lets out a hiss. His eyes turn a shade of red, even more vivid than before, and he tilts his head, his nose twitching.

"Blood." He grinds out the word, and my eyes widen when I realize what that means. "Tell me to stop."

He waits for me to say the word, looking more feral than I've ever seen him.

I swallow, then quickly say, "Bite me."

Lightning-fast, Archie tilts his head and sinks his fangs into my neck.

Archie

♥

The moment my fangs pierce her flesh, time stands still. I become acutely aware of every sound. The faint sound of the air-conditioning keeping the place cool. The rustling sheets as Janet arches her hips up, taking my cock deeper inside her. Her heart pounds double-time as I drink from her. And the best sound of all—her moans of ecstasy as I pleasure her with my cock and my fangs.

I slide out of her and then sink into her heat, pressing her into the soft mattress. She wiggles her hips beneath me, trying to urge me to fuck her, but I need to take things slowly. This is her first time, and I vow to make it good for her.

I focus on sipping her blood, so I don't take too much, and so I can prolong the pleasure I give her as I drink from her. Janet clenches around me, and I lift my head, removing my fangs.

Her metallic taste is still on my tongue, and I know I'm never going to be able to let her go. I thought I was ready to die, but Janet has shown me I'm just beginning to live.

"Please, Archie," she begs. "I need more."

I groan and start to move inside her, watching the pleasure on her face.

She wriggles against me, urging me on.

I try to keep my speed human-slow, letting her get used to the size of me. I can't believe I'm her first. That I'm the only man who's ever been inside this woman. That I am lucky enough to make her mine.

I run my fingers down her chest, over her breasts and her belly, and across her still sensitive clit.

"Archie," she groans, and I grin, showing her my fangs.

There's no fear in her eyes at the sight. Only desire.

"You feel so good," she moans.

"You feel better." Which has to be true, because this moment, right here, is the best I've felt in my very long existence by far. So good I can't imagine anything better.

I grasp Janet's hips, lifting them off the bed, so I can thrust deeper. I pick up the pace as she urges me on. She moans and arches against me. The pleasure builds in me, and I can't stop. I'm gripping her so hard, I'm probably leaving marks, but her moans of pleasure tell me she's loving every moment.

I hold on, wanting her to reach her pleasure first. I slip my hand between us again and run my thumb along her clit. She tightens around me, and I do it again, and again. When she screams, shuddering and squeezing me with her orgasm, I let myself go, joining her in bliss.

I wait for her to catch her breath. Then I lie on top of her, still half in her, and she strokes my hair.

"I wasn't too bad?" she asks. "For a first timer?"

"Too bad?" I take her face in my hands and meet her eyes. "You were amazing, my beautiful queen. I want to take you like that every day for the rest of our lives."

She blinks at me. "Really?"

"Really," I say, settling beside her and taking her in my arms. "I know we just met. And I know this is too soon..." I trail off as I try to find a way to put the glow in my chest into words. "Janet, until I met you, I thought soulmates were poppycock."

"Poppycock?" Janet's gaze drops down between my legs, and I feel myself growing hard again.

"Balderdash," I say.

"What?" Janet stares at me blankly.

"Poppycock means balderdash." I struggle to think of a more modern saying. "Nonsense."

"Oh…" she whispers.

"I thought authors made soulmates up, same as how they made up vampires needing to be invited in and not having a soul. At least, I assume we have a soul." I pull her closer. "We're definitely not cursed, just a different species than humans. But that's not what I was trying to say."

"It's not?"

"No." I shake my head. "I was trying to say that somehow, between the moment when you appeared on my front porch and this moment right here, I've fallen in love with you."

"Love?" she whispers, eyes wide.

I meet her eyes again and press my hand to her breastbone just over her heart. "You feel it too, don't you?" I ask. "That we were meant for one another."

"Soulmates…" she whispers.

I nuzzle her neck, resisting the urge to bite. "Exactly."

"I never thought I'd fall in love," she says quietly. "I didn't think there was a man out there for me."

I smile, flashing a fang. "No, not a man. A vampire."

She nods, eyes unfocused. I almost think she's fallen asleep, despite her somewhat uneven breathing and elevated heart rate, when she whispers, "I love you, too."

"You don't have to say it back if you're not ready. I'm willing to wait. As long as it takes. I'm immortal…" And that longing to walk into the sun and end my endless existence is completely gone. There's only one desire left—to stay by Janet's side for all eternity.

"I didn't know it could happen so fast," she says. Then, as if reading my mind, she adds, "But I can't imagine ever leaving your side."

I cover her lips with mine and pull her in for a luxurious kiss. I don't intend to take things further, but I'm already hard. I grab Janet's hips, but she pulls back.

"Archie… you'll live so much longer than me… I must be like a blip in your long life."

I sit up, ignoring our nakedness and the scent of our love-making. "I love you, Janet, and I want to be with you forever."

"Forever?" she asks, nibbling on her lip. "Do you mean I could… become a vampire?"

I nod.

"I don't know," she says. "I need my job to pay the bills, and I can't do it if I need to avoid the sun, and…"

"I've amassed some wealth in my long life. You wouldn't need to work, not unless you wanted to."

She nods. "What about Page? And my family? I see my aunt and cousins at Christmas, and I keep in touch with a few friends from library school. If I just disappeared…"

"You won't have to disappear. The cat can come with us, and you can still see your family, for a while at least." I take her hands in mine. "Let's make a life together."

A frown etches itself across her forehead as she thinks, and a heavy weight settles in the pit of my stomach. I need to say something, anything, to tip the scale and convince her to be mine.

"Food tastes better as a vampire," I blurt. "And sex feels more amazing as a vampire." I rack my brain for something else.

"Archie, I'm not going to turn into a vampire for the food and sex."

My heart sinks.

"I'm going to do it for you."

"Do you mean...?"

She nods. "Yes, Archie. Let's do it."

I pull her into a tight hug—but not too tight, since I'm acutely aware that she's still human. Though not for long. "I love you, my queen."

"I love you, too, Archie," she says, and pulls me to her for a kiss.

Epilogue: Janet

♥

"**F**aster, Archie," I shout as we race up the steps of the Eiffel Tower. They're the same words I shouted last night, and just thinking about it makes me want to get my vampire naked again.

Archie and I are the only ones at the Eiffel Tower at this time of night. The place is closed, but we slipped the guards a few hundred Euros—and slipped into their minds so they wouldn't remember our little super-speed adventure—so we don't have to worry about being arrested or exposing our kind.

Our kind. I smile as the words flit through my mind.

It's been two full years since Achibald LaVere turned me into a vampire. A split second for him, but a nice chunk of time for me to adjust, since I'm still living on human time. Archie says after the first hundred years, that will change, and the thought of being with him for all those years makes me smile. As does the fact that the two of us are in Paris, and that we have enough money to travel wherever we want, whenever we want. And that we can afford pet-friendly hotels that provide litter boxes and cat trees for Page.

I put on another burst of speed and race up the Eiffel Tower steps so fast they blur around me. Archie's footsteps pound behind me, keeping pace. As the older vamp, he can easily move faster, but he's enjoying the chase. And the reward that awaits us both when we get to the top.

I'm not even panting as I cover the last few steps and practically fly across the landing. My dress billows around my knees, and my fingers barely graze the railing before Archie spins me around and pins me with my back against it.

"Are you enjoying Paris, my queen?" he asks, his eyes dancing when they meet mine.

I nod, my gaze dropping down to his lips. The City of Love is the last thing on my mind.

"Is it everything you've hoped for?" he asks. He's smiling, but I catch something in his eyes. A hint of nerves.

"Is my vampire king actually worried?" I tease.

Silence.

Archie doesn't tease me back, or lean in to kiss me, or whisper sweet nothings in my ear. He stares at me as the warm evening air caresses my cold skin.

I take his hands in mine and smile up at him. "Archie, Paris is beautiful."

He raises an eyebrow. "You haven't even looked around."

He looks past my shoulder at the city sprawled beneath us, and I realize he's right. Coming here has been my dream since I first started working at my little library. It's what I've been saving up for all this time. And yet, being here, all I care about is the man standing in front of me. We might as well be back home for all the attention I've given the city of my dreams.

"It's hard to pay attention to anything else when I'm with you," I tell him softly, meaning every word. "I love you so much, Archie. You're all I can think about. And I don't care where we are, as long as we're together."

He shakes his head in mock disappointment, though I can see the amusement in his eyes. "How am I supposed to spoil my queen when she says things like that?"

"You don't," I tell him honestly. "I don't need spoiling. All I need is you."

I rise on tiptoe and press my lips against his. They're soft, and the kiss starts out gentle, but like it always does with us, it quickly turns all-consuming. Heat surges through my body, and in the time it takes Archie to lift my skirt, I'm already whimpering and pleading for him to take me.

As he pushes my beige panties aside and slides inside me, I throw my head back in ecstasy. I know it won't always be this hard and fast between us. Archie and I have been researching vampire fated mates, and it turns out we're not the only ones out there. We've learned that the fire between new mates is always all-consuming, but that eventually, we'll be able to take our time when we make love.

"When do you think that *eventually* will be?" I'd asked. We'd been in the stacks of the Lakeview city library above his kingdom, making love against a shelf of history books.

"Probably a few hundred years," Archie had whispered in my ear. "So not long at all."

I moan as the pleasure between us builds, but I can't help smiling at the thought of spending hundreds of years with the love of my life. Or maybe thousands.

"What has you smiling?" Archie pants as he slams inside me. "Is it Paris?"

I catch the hopeful tone in his voice and can't help grinning. "No. It's you."

I shatter around his cock and cry out a split second before Archie shouts his release. The sound echoes around us and disperses over the rooftops of Paris. And as I sag against the love of my life, I finally take in our surroundings. The bright city lights of the most romantic city on Earth.

"It's beautiful," I whisper, and I don't just mean Paris. I mean everything. The man who just brought me pleasure, my fated mate, my love. This place, and the dream life we're now living. And the future that stretches out before us, beautiful and filled with amazing experiences I can't wait to share with my king.

After we adjust our clothes, we turn to stare out over the city. Archie wraps an arm around me and pulls me into his side. He plants a soft kiss on my forehead. "I love you, Janet."

My heart swells as I stare up into his eyes. "I love you too, Archie. Forever and always."

***

Thank you for reading REVAMPING THE LIBRARIAN. If you'd like to see what other hijinks the cowriting duo, Mia Harlan and Cali Mann, get up to, grab FANGED AT FIRST SIGHT: Esme's been raised to hate vampires, but when a too-hot-to-handle vamp saves her life, she may just change her mind. One-click to read FANGED AT FIRST SIGHT: https://books2read.com/Fanged

Looking for more feel-good romance?

Peppermint by Cali Mann: "My men are trapped in the underworld and all I've got is a pair of ice skates and a letter." Read PEPPERMINT today: books2read.com/PeppermintSilverSkates

Her Pastry Shifters by Mia Harlan: "What's more delicious than three hot men who shift into pastries?" Get your copy of HER PAS-

TRY SHIFTERS now: books2read.com/Her-Pastry-Shifters

About the Authors

Cali Mann is the USA Today bestselling author of the Thornbriar Academy series. She writes paranormal romance, the sexy kind with hunky shifters, sexy vampires, and women who stand up for themselves. She learned romance by reading through her mother's entire romance collection in her teens, so she and romance go way back. When she's not writing, she spends her time streaming shows, playing video games, and pestering her two tuxedo cats. Sign up for Cali's newsletter for exclusive content and sneak peeks: https://calimann. substack.com/

Say hello to Cali online on her website at www.calimann.com, Facebook, or Instagram.

Mia Harlan is a USA Today & International Bestselling Author who writes quirky romance guaranteed to make you laugh. A librarian by day and author by night, she lives in Canada with her husband (who's definitely NOT a vampire) and their Mini Mortal (who doesn't have fangs). Sign up for Mia's Patreon for exclusive content and early access to future books: patreon.com/miaverse

You can follow Mia on Tiktok, Goodreads, and Bookbub.

Also By Cali Mann

Thornbriar Academy series

Lost

Found

Bound

Saved

Bloody Lucky (a Thornbriar Academy side story)

Beautiful & Deadly (Boxset)

Misfit of Thornbriar Academy series

Infiltrate

Destroy

Shifter Island

Uncursing Her Bears

Finding Their Mermaid

Hell-Baited Wolves series

Cowritten with Freya Black

Guarded by the Hellhounds

Called

Scorned

Unleashed

Charming Her Wolves (Boxset)

Silver Springs Shared World

Peppermint

Delphine

Cowritten with Elena Gray:

Mars

Standalones:

Dark Magic

Cowritten with Mia Harlan:

Reckless

Fanged at First Sight

Also By Mia Harlan

Shifter Bay

Enter a world like no other, and fall in love at first sight with unique, quirky shifters.

Her Donut Shifters

Her Pastry Shifters

Billionaire Rubber Duckie Shifter (coming soon)

Silver Springs

Lose yourself in a quirky, paranormal small town filled with magic and fated mates.

Amber

Amber: Deja Brew

Amber Goes Yeti

Amber's Christmas Surprise

Violet

Deflated (with Eva Delaney)

Violet: A Monster-ly Undercover Christmas

Wynter

Moonlit Nephrite (with Eva Delaney)

Tall, Dark, and Haunted (with Hanleigh Bradley)

Saturn (with Hanleigh Bradley)

Venus (with Hanleigh Bradley)

Neptune (with Hanleigh Bradley)

Beach Romance (Writing as Mia Sands)

Librarians find love at a beach resort in these spicy shorts.

Mile High Librarian

Mister Fit

Other

An Espresso Machine's Guide to Love and Mischief (with Eva Delaney)

Glow Sticks (with Sapphire Winters)

Paranormal Reverse Harem Romance Reader Challenge: A Coloring Book

Milton Keynes UK
Ingram Content Group UK Ltd.
UKHW010702240424
441619UK00004B/198

9 798224 972272